I SURVIVED

THE AMERICAN REVOLUTION, 1776

I SURVIVED

THE DESTRUCTION OF POMPEII, AD 79

THE BATTLE OF GETTYSBURG, 1863

THE GREAT CHICAGO FIRE, 1871

THE SAN FRANCISCO EARTHQUAKE, 1906

THE SINKING OF THE *TITANIC*, 1912

THE SHARK ATTACKS OF 1916

THE *HINDENBURG* DISASTER, 1937

THE BOMBING OF PEARL HARBOR, 1941

THE NAZI INVASION, 1944

THE ERUPTION OF MOUNT ST. HELENS, 1980

THE ATTACKS OF SEPTEMBER 11, 2001

HURRICANE KATRINA, 2005

THE JAPANESE TSUNAMI, 2011

THE JOPLIN TORNADO, 2011

I SURVIVED

THE AMERICAN REVOLUTION, 1776

by Lauren Tarshis

illustrated by Scott Dawson

Scholastic Inc.

Text copyright © 2017 by Lauren Tarshis

Illustrations copyright © 2017 Scholastic Inc.

Photos ©: p. vi: North Wind Picture Archives; p. 121: The New York Historical Society/Getty Images; p. 127: Charles Willson Peale/Dick S. Ramsay Fund/Brooklyn Museum (34.1178_SL3)

This book is being published simultaneously in hardcover by Scholastic Press.

ISBN 978-0-545-91973-9

10 9 8 7 6 5 4 3 2 1   17 18 19 20 21

Printed in the U.S.A.   40
First printing, September 2017
Designed by Yaffa Jaskoll

To Stefanie I. Dreyfuss, my friend

TO ALL BRAVE, HEALTHY, ABLE BODIED, AND WELL DISPOSED YOUNG MEN,

IN THIS NEIGHBOURHOOD, WHO HAVE ANY INCLINATION TO JOIN THE TROOPS,
NOW RAISING UNDER

GENERAL WASHINGTON,

FOR THE DEFENCE OF THE

LIBERTIES AND INDEPENDENCE

OF THE UNITED STATES,

Against the hostile designs of foreign enemies,

TAKE NOTICE,

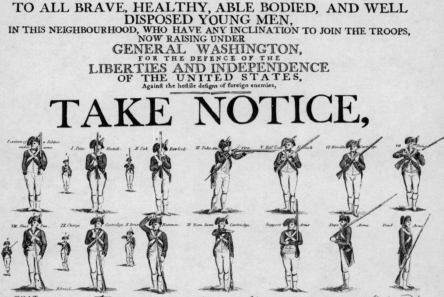

THAT _____ tuesday, wednsday Thursday friday and Saturday at Spotswood in _____ county, attendance will be given by Lieutenant Reating _____ with his music and recruiting party of _____ company in Major Mules Battalion of the 11th regiment of infantry, commanded by Lieutenant Colonel Aaron Ogden, for the purpose of receiving the enrollment of such youth of SPIRIT, as may be willing to enter into this HONOURABLE service.

The ENCOURAGEMENT at this time, to enlist, is truly liberal and generous, namely, a bounty of TWELVE dollars, an annual and fully sufficient supply of good and handsome cloathing, a daily allowance of a large and ample ration of provisions, together with SIXTY dollars a year in GOLD and SILVER money on account of pay, the whole of which the soldier may lay up for himself and friends, as all articles proper for his subsistance and comfort are provided by law, without any expence to him.

Those who may favour this recruiting party with their attendance as above, will have an opportunity of hearing and seeing in a more particular manner, the great advantages which these brave men will have, who shall embrace this opportunity of spending a few happy years in viewing the different parts of this beautiful continent, in the honourable and truly respectable character of a soldier, after which, he may, if he pleases return home to his friends, with his pockets FULL of money and his head COVERED with laurels.

GOD SAVE THE UNITED STATES.

CHAPTER 1

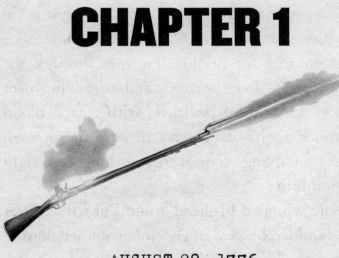

AUGUST 29, 1776
BROOKLYN, NEW YORK

Nathaniel Fox was too young to be fighting in the Revolutionary War. He was only eleven years old. But here he was on a blood-soaked battlefield in Brooklyn, New York. Thousands of British soldiers were on the attack. And Nate was sure that he was about to die.

Gunfire crackled through the air.

KI-crack!

Cannon blasts shook the ground.

Kaboom!

Already one of Nate's friends was lying dead in the dirt, shot through the heart. And now Nate was running for his life. He tore through the thick forest, dodging trees and stumbling over rocks. His mind swirled with fear. Blood pounded in his ears. And then came an even more terrifying sound: heavy footsteps right behind him.

Nate whipped his head around in panic. Over his shoulder, he saw an enormous soldier chasing after him. The man's musket was aimed at Nate's back. Attached to the gun's tip was a killing sword — a bayonet.

Nate ran faster, desperate to escape. But he could hear the man's pounding steps, and his grunting breaths.

"I'm not a soldier!" Nate wanted to scream.

But it was too late. The man was closing in.

Closer, closer, closer.

Nate braced himself for the killing stab. He was sure this was the end.

And then came an ear-shattering blast.

Boom!

Nate saw flames. A blinding light.

And then the world went black.

CHAPTER 2

Nate crawled along his uncle's vegetable garden, tugging up weeds and flicking away fat green worms. The burning sun cooked his back. His muscles ached from hours of work. But even worse was the sound of his uncle's voice, barking through the open dining room window. His uncle was talking about the war with England.

4

Nate peeked through the window. His uncle, Uriah Storch, was sitting at the fine wooden table. He was eating his noon meal with his best friend, Mr. Marston. Nate breathed in the delicious food smells. But there was nothing delicious about watching Storch gobble the leg of a roasted goose. Storch pretended to be a gentleman. But Nate had seen hogs with better manners.

"George Washington should be hanged!" Storch was saying, cracking the poor goose's bone with his large teeth.

George Washington was the commander of the American army. Most people in Connecticut loved General Washington. They called themselves Patriots, which meant they were rooting for the Americans to win the war.

But Storch and his pal were on England's side. Storch hated George Washington more than he hated the fleas that crawled around his curled white wig.

Storch turned toward the kitchen and bellowed, "More meat!"

Seconds later Eliza hurried in, carrying a silver platter piled high with fresh goose.

Eliza stood patiently while the men heaped food on their plates. She'd been up since dawn cooking this meal. But neither of the men thanked her, or even looked at her. Nate hated living here with Storch. But Eliza had it far worse. Nate was his nephew. Eliza was Storch's slave.

Nate caught Eliza's eye through the window. He pushed together his lips and puffed out his cheeks — his best Storch imitation. Eliza raised her eyebrow at Nate, a reminder that he'd better

6

watch himself. Storch was always looking for an excuse to give Nate a whack with his walking stick. He would not be happy to see Nate's blue eyes peering through the window.

Nate ducked away. He had hours of work left to do, but he needed a break from the heat. He went to a shady spot under the cherry tree and looked down at the Long Island Sound. He loved watching the ships sailing by.

Nate closed his eyes and pretended he was on one of those ships, heading out to the open sea. His mind filled up with the sounds of flapping sails and squawking seagulls. He imagined a cool sea breeze ruffling his hair. He could practically feel his father's strong hand resting on his shoulder.

Papa had been a ship's captain. After Nate's mama got sick and died, when Nate was just four, Papa started taking Nate along with him on his voyages. Nate grew up crisscrossing the ocean with Papa and his crews.

What a happy life!

Sure, not every kid would want to grow up on the sea. The creaking wooden sailing ships were crawling with rats. The stale, wormy biscuits could break your teeth. Nate's bed was a hammock hanging from the ceiling.

But none of that mattered. Because Nate was with Papa.

Nate pictured his father's green eyes flashing from under his old sailing cap, his black ponytail waving in the wind. He'd wrap his arm around Nate's shoulder as they stood on the deck, looking out at the endless ocean.

"You never know what's ahead," Papa would say, his eyes brimming with excitement.

But now a wave of sadness crashed over Nate.

Papa died almost two years ago, while they were sailing home from a trip to the Caribbean islands. The voyage had been smooth, with steady winds, a glassy sea, and a crew of ten men. Nate's favorite crew member was Paul Dobbins, a joking eighteen-year-old with bright red hair and a gap-toothed grin. He'd sailed with Papa before, and had always treated Nate like a favorite brother.

They had been halfway through their three-week voyage home when they sailed into the path of a wicked storm. It came out of nowhere, a ferocious squall with swirling black clouds, pounding rain, and lightning that tore open the sky. The winds blew like dragon's breath. Waves crashed over the deck.

Papa and the crew worked frantically, sliding across rain-soaked decks and pushing through the whipping winds. Giant, twisting waves spun the ship like a toy.

The crew managed to take down the sails. But then a twenty-foot wave grabbed hold of Papa and swept him off the deck. In a blink, he was swallowed up by the sea — and gone forever.

Suddenly Nate was an orphan with just one living relative in the world: the uncle that Papa had always hated. Papa had stayed away from Storch, a man as mean as he was rich. Storch was the last person Papa would have wanted Nate to live with.

But where else could Nate go?

Paul had promised to stay in touch. He'd hugged Nate tight and sworn he'd always look after him. "We're blood, you and me," he'd said.

But that was just talk. Nate hadn't heard a peep from Paul in two years, and he had no idea why.

Nate knew he should be thankful that Storch gave him a home. Plenty of orphans ended up as beggars. At least Nate had family to take him in. Except Storch had never treated Nate like family. A stray dog was more like it.

It was Eliza who'd made sure Nate knew he wasn't alone in the world. During Nate's first months with Storch, he was tortured by nightmares. He'd wake up and find Eliza sitting by his bed. She'd be gripping his hand tight, like she'd just pulled him out of the churning sea. She was Nate's family now.

Nate stood there under the cherry tree, his mind swirling with sad memories. He was so distracted he didn't hear the footsteps creeping up behind him.

Something poked his back. A voice growled. "Back to work or I'll chop you up!"

CHAPTER 3

Nate stood very still.

"Are you a pirate?" Nate asked.

"Yes," the voice said. "A pie-wit. I want my tweasure."

Nate's heart lifted up.

He whirled around to face his attacker: three-year-old Theo, Eliza's little boy. He was waving his pirate sword — a spindly stick from the cherry tree.

Theo was supposed to be napping — and out of Storch's sight. But here he was, wide awake.

"You are very fierce!" Nate told his friend.

Theo stood proudly, his brown eyes gleaming like polished gold. He'd been wild about pirates for months now, ever since Nate started telling him stories about his adventures at sea.

Theo waved his stick sword.

"Aargh!" he shouted out in his most pirate-like voice.

Nate grabbed Theo around the waist and picked him up. Theo's happy giggles rose up, whooshing over Nate like a breeze.

Seconds later Eliza came rushing out of the house, her skirt swirling around her shoes. Eliza had Theo's same dark brown skin and big, bright eyes. But unlike Theo, Eliza wasn't smiling.

"You both need to hush!" she warned, looking toward the house. "You know what he could do if he hears!"

He, of course, was Storch. He had no patience for giggling, and even less for Theo himself.

Eliza's worst nightmare was that Storch would sell Theo, just like he'd sold Eliza's husband, Gregory, a few months before Nate arrived. Eliza rarely talked about Gregory — it hurt her too

much, Nate knew. But she had told Nate a few things about her husband — that he was joyful like Theo and had those same bright eyes, that not one hour went by without her missing him.

What a fool Nate was, getting Theo all riled up!

Luckily Storch was probably too busy cursing George Washington to notice Theo's giggles.

"Mama," Theo said very quietly. "I a pie-wit."

Eliza's eyes softened, and she and Nate shared a little smile.

"Even pirates have to be quiet," Eliza said, kissing Theo on the nose. "Or they get into trouble."

Storch's voice bellowed from the house.

"Cake!"

"I'll keep this pirate out of trouble," Nate promised.

Eliza rushed inside to serve Storch and his friend.

Theo put his face close to Nate's.

"Tell a pie-wit story!" Theo begged. "Tell about Slash!"

Slash was Slash O'Shea, the greatest living pirate. Nate had grown up hearing Papa's stories about Slash. And Nate had shared most of them with Theo. Slash got his name from the dagger strapped to the stump where his hand used to be.

Some pirates were nothing more than low-life thieves. They captured ships and stole everything they could. They murdered anyone who got in their way. Not Slash. He'd never killed a man. And he gave some of his treasure away — mostly to orphans. He'd sneak into cities disguised in ragged beggar's clothes and hand out gold coins to kids living on the streets.

"I'll tell you a Slash story later," said Nate. "How about a song?"

A grin spread across Theo's face.

He loved when Nate sang shanties — the songs sailors crooned as they did their work. Nate sang Theo one of Papa's favorites, about the sun rising up over the sea.

Soon enough Theo's eyes were closed.

Nate gently pried the stick-sword from Theo's hand. He lifted his little friend up and carried him to a soft patch of grass. Then Nate went back to his weeds and worms.

Storch and Marston had finished their cake and were puffing on cigars.

They were still talking about the war.

"Don't worry, my friend; this war will be over soon," Storch was saying. "The king sent hundreds of ships. The big battle is coming any day. Washington and his army of traitors will soon be crushed."

Marston nodded his jowly face in agreement.

Nate didn't pay much attention to the war. He understood what it was about: whether the thirteen American colonies should stay a part of England or become a country of their own.

He remembered the late-night talks on Papa's ships. Nate would lie in his hammock and listen to Papa and the men griping about England and King George.

There was no mention of a war back then. Most of the men were proud that America was part of England, the most powerful country on Earth. But they hated paying so many taxes — the extra money England made the colonists pay when they bought things like tea and paper. They'd started to see King George as a bully who didn't care about the people who lived in the colonies.

Their fiery discussions would last deep into the night. Nate would struggle to stay awake. He never wanted to miss a word of what they were saying.

But now Nate didn't care about King George.

It didn't matter to him who won the war. Whatever happened, he was pretty sure Eliza and Theo would still be slaves. Papa would still be gone. And Nate would be stuck here, pulling up Storch's weeds.

Nate stopped listening to Storch and Marston. Time crawled by. The front door banged open and Mr. Marston walked out to his waiting carriage. Storch stood outside and waved good-bye as he puffed on a cigar.

It was right then that Nate realized that Theo wasn't asleep in the grass anymore. Nate scanned the yard until he spotted the little boy. He was next to the house, just a few yards from Storch. Theo had found a new pirate sword — an enormous stick, almost as big as he was. He was spinning around and around like a top. The stick whipped around with him.

Storch had his back turned and couldn't see Theo.

Just then Theo stumbled. The stick slipped from his hand. It flew surprisingly fast, like a spear.

And it was heading right for Storch's head.

Nate's heart stopped. He opened his mouth to scream out a warning.

But it was too late.

Thwack!

The stick smacked Storch right on the back of his head.

He cursed in pain. And then Nate's uncle fell to the ground like an empty sack.

CHAPTER 4

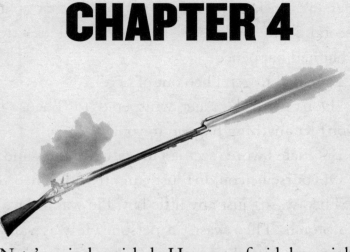

Nate's mind swirled. He was afraid he might vomit. It wasn't Storch's moans of pain that sickened him.

It was knowing what would happen to Theo.

Storch would sell him for sure. Eliza would lose him forever, just like she'd lost her husband, Gregory.

Nate rushed over to Theo, who was trying to hide behind the cherry tree.

Nate lifted Theo up and hugged him close.

Eliza was on the porch now, bending down to help Storch.

Eliza looked up. She spotted Nate and Theo. Her eyes locked with Nate's. And in that split second Nate could see she understood exactly what had happened.

Nate had to get Theo out of here!

"Don't worry!" Nate whispered to Theo. "I won't let anything happen to you."

But Nate's words seemed to scatter in the wind.

Of course he couldn't just run off with Theo.

Theo wasn't just any little boy. He was a slave. To Storch, Theo wasn't a person. He was valuable property. Storch wouldn't just let him go. He'd hire slave catchers. He'd offer a fat reward. He'd never stop looking.

There was nothing Nate could to do help Theo. Unless . . .

An idea flickered in Nate's mind like a little flame.

Storch hadn't seen Theo throw the stick, had he? His back had been turned.

What if Nate could trick Storch into thinking someone *else* had thrown the stick?

Then Theo would be safe.

Nate put Theo down.

"Run behind the barn," Nate whispered. "Never tell anyone what happened with that stick."

"You come, too." Theo said, clinging to Nate's arm.

"Soon," Nate said, struggling to keep his voice steady.

He hated lying to Theo. But he had no choice.

Theo turned and dashed away.

Nate stood up. With clenched fists and shaking legs, Nate made his way to where Storch was now sitting up. Eliza was pressing a rag to his bleeding head.

"I'm sorry, sir," he said. "It was an accident. The stick slipped from my hand."

"Nate," Eliza whispered.

Storch struggled to his feet, glaring at Nate with fury.

If Storch's eyes had been cannons, they would have blasted Nate into the sky.

He lunged forward.

Smack!

He slapped Nate across the face. Nate staggered

21

back. His face felt like he had been scalded with boiling water.

Tears sprang into Nate's eyes — tears of relief.

That slap meant that Storch believed him. That Theo was safe, at least for now.

But Nate was not.

Storch lunged forward and grabbed Nate by the throat. His hands were like iron claws. With his bulging eyes and blood-smeared face, Storch looked like a sea monster from Nate's worst nightmares.

Nate struggled but couldn't break free from the choking grip.

Eliza screamed, but the voice inside Nate's mind screamed louder.

He's going to kill me!

With his last ounce of strength, Nate whipped his arm up and bashed his fist into the side of Storch's head.

Storch lost his grip and fell back.

Nate took one last look at Eliza.

"Go," she mouthed.

Nate turned and ran.

CHAPTER 5

JULY 12, 1776
JUST BEFORE DAWN
NORWALK, CONNECTICUT

Nate's eyes snapped open.

Hideous pictures flashed through his mind —
a blood-streaked face, clawlike hands grabbing
for his throat.

He blinked hard to end this nightmare, to
shake himself awake.

But then Nate understood — he *was* awake.

He was hiding out in the woods about three

23

miles from Storch's house. This is where he'd wound up after his breathless run. He'd sat here under the trees for hours, in a kind of numb shock, trying to figure out what to do.

Somehow he must have fallen asleep.

It was now pitch dark. Strange sounds rose up around him. Clicks and buzzes and hoots, the rustling of invisible wings and paws. His jaw throbbed. His neck felt swollen and bruised. But even worse was the loneliness. He felt like a castaway clinging to a barrel in a stormy ocean.

He'd made a giant mistake, he realized, fighting back tears.

He had to go back to Storch's — to Eliza and Theo.

He stood up and started to make his way through the woods.

Storch would be calmer now, Nate told himself. And whatever Storch might to do to him, he'd have to take it. Because what choice did he have?

He didn't have a single coin in his pocket or a scrap of food to eat. He was just a boy, alone in the world.

But then as Nate walked along, he thought about another boy who had once been by himself.

The pirate Slash O'Shea.

Nate slowed down as he remembered the stories Papa had told him about when Slash was a kid.

He'd been born in London, England. His parents had died before he was five years old. He wasn't called Slash yet — back then he was called Jonathan. With his parents gone, he wound up in a filthy orphanage, more like a prison than a home for helpless kids. The food was barely fit for pigs. The beatings were brutal. Finally young Jonathan couldn't take it. When he was ten years old, he ran away.

He must have been terrified, Nate thought. Like Nate was now.

But there was no way he'd go back to that wretched orphanage.

Jonathan got himself a job on a ship, as a cabin boy. He'd sailed away. And he never looked back.

Nate pictured a boy standing on the deck of a big sailing ship.

The boy's face became clearer . . . until it became Nate's own face.

Nate blinked. Something inside him shimmered. Suddenly the night didn't seem so dark.

If young Slash could go to sea, why couldn't he?

Sure, Nate was too young — Papa wouldn't hire cabin boys who were younger than fourteen.

But Nate was bigger and taller than most eleven-year-olds. And Papa had taught him to work harder than sailors twice his age.

Nate quickened his step as he made his plan.

New York City was about fifty miles south of here. He'd go to Norwalk Harbor. There were always boats heading down to New York City, loaded up with vegetables or oysters or hogs to sell. Nate would hide out on one of those boats. If the winds and currents were strong, he would be in New York City by the afternoon. The city had one of the busiest harbors in the colonies, with merchant ships heading to the Caribbean and

Europe and all corners of the world. There had to be at least one captain willing to give Nate a chance.

Nate could practically feel Papa's hand on his back, pushing him along. He saw Theo in his mind, with his bright and hopeful eyes.

And remembered the last word Eliza had said to him.

"Go."

He made it to the harbor several hours later. The docks were already crowded with sailors and fishermen preparing for the day.

And for once Nate lucked out. At the end of the dock was the sailing ship *Valerie*. It made weekly runs to New York City, Nate knew. And its deck was already loaded up with baskets and crates heaped with corn and potatoes and cherries. The sails were up. The ship was about to leave!

There were only three men working on the small ship. They were too busy working to notice when he slipped on board. He scurried across the deck and hid himself between two big baskets of corn.

A few minutes later sailors pushed the boat away from the dock.

And with a whoosh of wind, Nate was on his way.

CHAPTER 6

Nate stayed very still in his hiding place. His empty stomach churned with worry. Panicked thoughts spun around his brain. Would he ever see Theo and Eliza again? What if Eliza had to do all of Nate's work now? How would she watch over Theo?

The rocking of the ship calmed him some. He listened to the familiar sounds — the *swoosh, crack* of the sails, the *creak, creak* of the wood, the twang of the sailors' voices. Bright pictures filled up his mind, memories of visiting New York City with Papa. Some of their voyages had started from there. And Papa always left a day or two for them to explore before they set sail.

New York City wasn't as big as Philadelphia, but it had twenty-five thousand people — twenty-five thousand! That was more people than Boston or Charleston. New York was dirty and smelly like every city Nate had ever visited. Garbage rotted in the alleys. Piles of horse dung steamed in the streets.

But Papa always said New York was the prettiest city in the colonies, and Nate agreed. The wide streets were lined with tall elm trees. Gardens were bursting with sweet-smelling flowers that almost covered up the garbage stink.

Nate loved the sidewalk puppet shows and jugglers who spun torches on the street corners. Papa would tip his cap at the ladies swishing by in their bright dresses.

Best of all was the food — suppers of juicy rabbit stew and gooey boiled puddings and buttery dumplings that slid down Nate's throat. One restaurant was so fancy they actually gave Nate and Papa each a fork. A fork! Even most rich people like Storch ate with a knife and their fingers. But Nate and Papa figured out that strange new tool pretty quick.

Nate's mind flashed with memories of Papa as the *Valerie* sailed down the twisting coastline of Connecticut and New York. He shut up his grumbling stomach by sneaking a few ears of corn.

The sun was high in the sky when they came to Manhattan — the island of New York. Most of the long and skinny island was wild land: rolling green hills and forests and marshes with a just a few orchards and farms. It looked so quiet and peaceful. It was hard for Nate to imagine that busy New York City was just a few miles down, on the island's southern tip.

But slowly the city came into view. Nate spotted crooked rooftops, the wharves jutting into the river, and too many church steeples to count.

The *Valerie* sailed toward the bottom of the island and turned into one of the wharves. Nate didn't bother waiting until the *Valerie* was completely stopped. The moment it was close to the dock, he sprang up. With a few steps and a leap he was off the boat. One of the *Valerie*'s sailors swore in surprise as Nate streaked past him. But Nate was gone before anyone could stop him.

He ran down the dock, zigzagging around baskets and barrels and coils of ropes. There were only a few dockworkers milling around, and no big merchant ships. That was a little strange; last time there were too many ships to count. The docks had been packed with sailors from all over the world, lugging crates and barrels and shouting out in languages he'd never heard before.

But Nate wasn't worried. He'd probably come into a different wharf this time. It shouldn't be hard to find where the merchant ships were docked.

A thrill rushed through him as he left the waterfront, his boots clicking against the city's familiar cobblestone streets.

He'd made it!

But as he plunged into the city, his excitement drained away.

Why were some of the streets deserted?

Why were some of the streets blocked off by big dirt walls?

He saw no puppet shows, no ladies in swishing dresses, no fancy coaches clattering through the streets. Most of the stores were boarded up.

On one block the only people around were men — soldiers, Nate realized. He could tell they were American soldiers by their plain clothes. British soldiers were famous for their brass-buttoned red coats — that's where the name "Redcoat" came from. They wore spiffy leather hats, bright white shirts, and belts with brass buckles.

American soldiers had no uniforms. Most of them wore cheap felt three-cornered hats and frontier shirts that tied at the collar. "Those rebel soldiers look like scarecrows," Storch had said. Looking around, Nate thought Storch wasn't far off. Most of the men wore dusty trousers and work shirts. Their weapons were beat-up muskets or rifles.

The deeper into the city Nate walked, the more soldiers he saw. Most were hard at work. At the end of the street, dozens of men were building another big dirt wall. Farther down Nate saw three men pulling a cart carrying a huge cannon.

What was happening here?

The hairs on the back of Nate's neck prickled up. Nate suddenly remembered what Storch and Marston had been talking about yesterday as they ate their goose. Nate hadn't been paying close attention. But now Storch's words came back to him, as though he were right next to Nate, barking in his ear.

"The king sent hundreds of ships."

"The big battle is coming any day."

"Washington and his army of traitors will soon be crushed."

Nate figured Storch and Marston had been talking about Boston. As far as he knew, that's where most of the fighting had been.

But now Nate realized they must have been talking about New York City.

No wonder the docks had been mostly empty.

No wonder the streets were deserted.

There had to be thousands of soldiers here.

Most of the people living here must have left.

And that's when Nate fully understood what he'd done.

He'd escaped from Storch.

And he'd landed smack in the middle of the war.

CHAPTER 7

3:15 P.M.

Nate charged back to the waterfront.

His best hope was to catch the *Valerie* back to Connecticut. He'd figure out what to do when he got there. If he couldn't sneak onto the *Valerie* like last time, he'd beg the captain to take him. He'd offer to scrub the decks, carry out the dead rats — anything!

But Nate was too late.

He reached the dock just as the *Valerie* was sailing away.

He tore down the dock, yelling.

"Stop! Wait! Come back!"

But the sailors couldn't hear him. And even if they could, Nate knew the captain wouldn't turn the ship around for some nobody kid.

Now what would Nate do?

He stared out into the harbor, as though the answer might be floating in the water. And that's when he spotted them: two enormous sailing ships. They were coming from the south and seemed to be heading right for the city.

Nate's heart lifted up: Maybe he'd find a job after all!

But as the ships came closer, he realized they were not regular sailing ships like Papa's. They were bigger. They rose proudly out of the water, each with twelve sparkling white sails gleaming in the sun.

As they turned slightly, Nate saw that both ships had small square openings along the sides. And poking out of each square was the black muzzle of a cannon. They were like gigantic black serpents, peering out from their caves.

Flags of England flapped from the ships' masts. They were British warships!

Nate stared with a mix of fear and fascination, like the time he found a scorpion in his hammock. All his life he'd been hearing stories about the British navy. It was the mightiest on Earth, with hundreds of warships prowling the seas.

The greatest British warship of them all were called men-of-war — floating cities that could hold a thousand men and almost a hundred big cannons. Each cannon could blast a twenty-four-pound ball that would streak through the air faster than a person could blink.

There was no weapon on Earth as powerful as a big cannon.

Nate knew it took five men to load and fire each one. One ball could punch through a stone fortress wall. It could rip through a line of soldiers. It could turn a house to rubble. It could blow a hole in an enemy warship, dooming it to an underwater grave.

But the crew of a big warship didn't just fire off one cannonball at a time. They fired dozens of cannons at once, unleashing a crushing wave of metal balls. A man-of-war could destroy a city within hours.

Nate's blood turned cold as he watched the two warships stream around the southern tip of the city.

A crowd of American soldiers had joined Nate on the dock.

They shouted out curses and shook their fists.

And then a thundering explosion shook the ground.

Kaboom!

The explosion rattled Nate's bones — and almost sent him leaping into the water in fear.

But then he realized that the blast hadn't come from either of the British ships.

Across the river, in Brooklyn, big puffs of gray smoke rose up from a hilltop. When the curtain of smoke cleared, Nate could see ten cannons lined up in a row.

Kaboom!
Kaboom!
Kaboom!

They blasted away at the British ships.

And then came blasts from somewhere closer — on this side of the river. The Americans must have put cannons all around the city.

Soldiers were crowding the docks now. Two men stood behind Nate. They screamed out insults to the British ships.

"Putting on a little show for us, you devils?" one jeered.

"We'll blast you up to the moon!"

The American cannons thundered and boomed. The air was filled with the sharp metal stink of gunpowder smoke.

Soldiers whooped and cheered after every blast.

Kaboom!

"Huzzah!"

Kaboom!

"Huzzah!"

None of the American cannonballs hit the ships; each splashed down harmlessly in the river.

But the soldiers didn't seem to care.

They roared and taunted.

"Sink those cowards!"

But then Nate noticed that the bigger of the British warships had slowed down.

A tongue of flame flicked out of one of its cannons.

Kaboom!

An odd sizzling sound filled the sky overhead. Someone screamed. And then,

Crash!

A cannonball came down, smashing a house just a few yards from where Nate stood. The ground shook. Shards of wood rained down. A man shouted out.

"Run!"

CHAPTER 8

Nate took off, joining the stampede of terrified soldiers rushing away from the docks. He ended up alone in an alley, huddling in the doorway of a stone building. He knew trying to hide was useless. No building would protect him from the force of a cannonball. But he couldn't just stand out in the street. He squeezed himself tighter into the doorway and tried not to think about the gruesome stories Papa's men used to tell, about men who'd had their heads blown off by cannonballs.

What a fool Nate was! He'd never make it out here on his own!

He wasn't tough like Slash O'Shea.

When Slash was just fourteen, the merchant ship he worked on was destroyed in a storm. Only a few men survived, including Slash. And what did he do next? He joined the British navy. England was in the middle of a huge war with France and Spain. Slash was stationed on a man-of-war, on the cannon deck. He was a powder monkey, which meant it was his job to rush heavy bags of explosive gunpowder to the men loading the cannons.

Powder monkeys had to be small and fast like real monkeys — and as brave as lions. Because cannons didn't just kill the enemy. Sudden sparks, too much gunpowder . . . any small mistake could cause an accidental explosion. It was one of those fiery accidents that left Slash without his right hand. After that, the navy didn't want him anymore.

But Slash didn't curl up like a little shrimp.

No! He went on to be the greatest pirate ever!

Thinking about Slash calmed Nate down a bit, and put that strong, shimmering feeling inside his chest again.

Nate closed his eyes and pictured Papa's face. He tried to imagine Eliza's hand gripping his.

When Nate finally opened his eyes, the explosions had faded. The smoke had mostly cleared. Those British warships must have sailed away. Nate unpeeled himself from the stone wall. Now he just wanted to get out of this battlefield. And if he couldn't escape on a boat, he'd just have to walk.

The whiff of gunpowder still prickled Nate's nose. But the danger seemed to have passed. The soldiers on the streets were back to work with their shovels and axes. Nate walked north, hoping to find the road out of the city. He passed a big lawn that had been turned into a huge army camp. Every inch of grass was covered with tents — row after crooked row of the grimiest, droopiest tents Nate had ever seen.

Nate wove through a crowd of soldiers building an enormous wall out of dirt and rocks.

A man's voice shouted out from somewhere behind him.

"Nate!"

Nate ignored it. There had to be dozens of Nathaniels in this city.

But then the voice shouted out again.

"Nathaniel Fox!"

Nate's heart stopped.

His mind spun until he understood who it had to be: one of Storch's men!

His wretched uncle had a whole crew of

muscled bullies he hired to collect money from people who owed him. And now one of those men had tracked Nate down. He was going to drag him back to Storch for more beatings.

Nate took off in a panic.

He sprinted across the street.

He had just made it when a strong hand grabbed hold of the back of his shirt.

Nate wriggled and squirmed until he wrenched himself free. He whirled around and raised his fists, ready to fight.

He lifted his chin and stared dead-on into the face of the man chasing him.

And then Nate's mouth fell open in shock.

It was a young soldier with a goofy, gap-toothed smile.

A mop of bright red curls spilled out from under a crumpled green triangle hat.

Before Nate could say anything, the man grabbed Nate into a crushing, joyful hug.

It was his old friend from Papa's crew: Paul Dobbins.

CHAPTER 9

Paul let go of Nate and stepped back. His smile had fallen away. Now his expression was almost angry, like Nate had hurt him somehow.

"I sent you at least ten letters!" Paul said. "I rode in a wagon for two days to get to your uncle's house. And when I got there, he told me you wouldn't see me. He slammed the door right in my face!"

Nate stood there in shock.

Storch was a lying, evil rat! He'd made Nate believe that his only old friend in the world had forgotten about him!

Tears burned Nate's eyes.

"I didn't know," he said, barely choking out the words.

Paul looked surprised at first. But his eyes drifted down to Nate's neck, which still hurt from Storch's strangling attack.

Paul's face turned white.

"Where did you get those bruises?" he said softly. "Did he . . ."

Nate hadn't seen himself in a mirror. But from Paul's horrified expression, Nate realized he must look worse than he imagined. Those angry bruises told Paul everything he needed to know about life with Storch.

"Good Lord, Nate," Paul whispered. "If I had known . . ."

Nate looked away so Paul wouldn't see his tears. But Paul was crying, too. And anyway, Nate wasn't crying about Storch — he wouldn't waste a tear on that snake-hearted beast. Nate was crying because he'd let himself lose faith in Paul.

Neither cried for long. Paul put his hands on Nate's shoulders. He leaned close.

"Well," he said. "We found each other, didn't we?"

They sat down in a shady spot near the tents. Paul peeled off his ugly green hat and placed it carefully on the ground.

"My lucky charm," he said.

Nate tried not to stare at Paul, but he kept thinking of the devilish teenager who'd clowned around on Papa's ships. He'd sneak vinegar into the men's canteens. He'd taught the ship's parrot to cuss in French. Nobody drove Papa and his men crazier — or made them laugh harder.

But now Paul's eyes looked serious and thoughtful. He listened closely as Nate told him about Storch, and how Eliza and Theo had become like family to him. He explained how he'd fled from Storch and had hoped to find a job on a ship.

Paul shook his head. "Hardly any ships coming

or going from New York City these days. The British attack is coming any day."

British warships had been streaming into the harbor all month, Paul said. Each one was packed tight with Redcoats. There were hundreds of ships here already, and tens of thousands of soldiers. The ships were anchored about eight miles from here, off Staten Island.

"Those two warships today gave us just a little hint of what's to come," Paul said. "They just wanted to give us a little scare, and catch us by surprise. Next time we'll be ready."

Paul told Nate that he'd been in the army for more than eighteen months, and stationed here in New York City since May. Before that he'd been living on his family's farm in northern Connecticut.

"I figured you'd gone back to sea," Nate said.

Paul shook his head, and a shadow passed across Paul's face. "I couldn't even look at the ocean. Not after . . ."

Nate finished the sentence in his mind.

After we lost Papa.

He and Nate were quiet for moment.

And then Paul went on. He told Nate about his life on the farm, how he'd loved being with his parents but had nearly gone crazy with boredom.

"The chickens never laughed at my jokes," he said.

Paul wanted an adventure. He thought about heading out west, to the wilds of Ohio.

But then, in April of 1775, everything changed.

That was when the first battle broke out between British and American troops, in and around the Massachusetts towns of Lexington and Concord.

The Revolutionary War had begun. Within a week, Paul had joined the fight.

"I had no idea what it meant to be a soldier," Paul said. "The first time I fired a musket, I almost blew my hand off."

He held out his thumb. It looked like the tip had been gnawed off by a barracuda.

Paul chuckled.

"But I had to learn pretty quick," Paul said,

serious again. That's because just about seven weeks later, he found himself in the bloody Battle of Bunker Hill.

"I almost didn't make it out of that one alive," he said quietly.

And then Paul told Nate the story of how he almost died on a hill outside of Boston.

CHAPTER 10

"It was two months after Lexington and Concord — June 1775," Paul began.

Almost exactly one year ago.

"I marched from Connecticut to Boston with about twenty other men from my town. It took a week — a hundred miles. My feet nearly fell off."

They joined about two thousand other American soldiers camped outside Boston.

Boston was the headquarters for the British army in America, Paul explained. There were six thousand Redcoats stationed there, and they'd taken over the city.

"The people of Boston were like prisoners. British soldiers moved into any house they wanted. There wasn't enough food. Shops were shut down. It was so bad. We had to do something to get the British out."

There was no American army yet. But each town in the colonies had a militia — a small group of volunteer fighters. Few of those men had ever fought in a war before.

"We were all just regular fellows — farmers, bakers, shopkeepers, shoemakers, sailors. Some of us didn't even know how to shoot."

And this ragtag group was about to battle the most powerful army in the world.

Paul and the other men knew all about the Redcoats. They were experienced fighters.

The British carried modern muskets. And their muskets had extra killing power — a sharp sword attached to the end — a bayonet.

"We heard that the British shoot first. And if you don't die from a musket ball to your gut, they'll finish you off with a quick stab in the heart with a bayonet."

Nate flinched.

The night before the battle, the Americans had been warned that thousands of British troops were on their way. Paul spent the night frantically helping to build fortifications — dirt walls and ditches that could protect them from musket fire.

"We worked all night," he said.

And then, just after dawn, the British attacked.

"We could hear them before we could see them," Paul said. "Their battle drums make a terrible sound."

Paul leaned forward. His voice dropped to a husky whisper.

"*RAT, tat, tat, tat, tat.*

RAT, tat, tat, tat, tat.

RAT, tat, tat, tat, tat."

The hairs on the back of Nate's neck stood up.

"Then came the cannon explosions. British warships had sailed into the river below us, and were blasting us nonstop with cannonballs."

"I was in one of the ditches — a trench. Somehow a big rock had gotten into my boot. I bent down to get it out. And the second I lowered my head, something huge went screaming over it."

"A cannonball?" Nate gasped.

"At least a twenty-pounder," Paul said. "It knocked my hat off. It could have taken off my head!"

He patted the ugly green hat next to him. "I always knew this was my lucky hat. I never go anywhere without it."

Paul took a deep breath.

"I was terrified. I just wanted to run away."

"But you didn't run," Nate guessed.

"No," Paul said. "It's amazing that none of us did.

"We were high up on that hill," Paul went on. "That's always where you want to be in a battle. On the high ground. It's easier to knock out your enemies when they're coming up a hill. And we were dug in — protected by our dirt walls and trenches.

"The drums got louder."

The British army finally appeared — four thousand Redcoat soldiers, marching in endless lines. They started up the hill.

"But we didn't shoot. Our plan was to wait until the British were close — close enough to see their eyes. And then we'd all shoot at once."

The British came closer, and closer.

Finally the order came.

"Fire!"

KI-crack! KI-crack! KI-crack! KI-crack!

Thousands of musket balls flew through the air.

"Hundreds of Redcoats fell. We Americans ducked behind our defenses and reloaded. Then we fired again."

KI-crack! KI-crack! KI-crack! KI-crack!

"The Redcoats sent up three waves of soldiers. And then the battle was over."

Paul took a deep breath, like he'd been running. Nate's own heart was pounding. It took him a moment to remember that they weren't on that bloody hill outside Boston. They were in New York City, sitting together in the grass.

"So you won the battle?" Nate asked excitedly.

"No," Paul said.

"You lost?" Nate asked, confused.

"Not really. We ran out of gunpowder. We had to retreat — escape down the back end of the hill. We didn't free Boston. So no. We definitely didn't win.

"But we didn't lose, either. More than a thousand Redcoats were killed or hurt that day. We lost about three hundred, not nearly as many as we thought we would."

But there was more.

"And we showed that Americans are willing to fight the most powerful army in the world. We showed that we can hold our ground."

As Paul kept talking, Nate realized how much he didn't know about the war. Lexington and Concord and Bunker Hill had just been the beginning. The Americans had lost a big battle up in Quebec, Canada. But they beat the British in a fight down in South Carolina. And this past March, the Americans finally drove the British out of Boston.

And then came the most shocking news: America wasn't part of England anymore. Not really. Just last week, on July 4, 1776, leaders of the American colonies signed a letter to King George. It had an important-sounding name: the Declaration of Independence.

"Our captain read it to us a few nights ago. I can't remember the fancy words, but basically it said that the American colonies are joining together to make a brand-new country, a free country: the United States of America.

"That's what this war is about. We are fighting for our new country."

And the biggest battle was about to happen right here — in New York.

Paul leaned forward. His eyes were flickering with excitement.

"So you'll join us?"

"The army?" Nate asked.

Now Paul had to be kidding — or crazy.

Nate couldn't fight in a war. He was only eleven years old!

But Paul was dead serious. And he wasn't

saying Nate should be a soldier — he'd have to be at least fourteen for that.

"I need to talk to the captain," Paul said. "He's been looking for a camp helper."

"He'd let me stay here?" Nate asked.

"I bet he would."

Nate thought of what Papa used to say as they would stand together on the deck of his ship, looking out over the ocean. "You never know what's ahead."

Papa was right.

Barely a day ago, Nate had been running for his life. And now here he was with his oldest friend in the world. He was going to be a part of George Washington's army.

Nate barely realized that he was smiling, and nodding.

"Looks like your answer is yes," Paul said.

CHAPTER 11

The days at the army camp started at dawn, when the drummers sounded the wake-up song. Nate chopped wood, dug trenches, and hauled water. By the end of the day, his muscles quivered like pudding. His hands were covered with bloody blisters. At night he'd collapse into his little droopy tent next to Paul's.

At first Nate felt himself under the watchful glare of Captain Marsh. He was the gruff and unsmiling head of the Connecticut 5th, Paul's army company. Captain Marsh made it clear from the start that he had doubts about hiring a boy so young.

"This is the army," he'd told Paul. "Not a nursery."

Nate's cheeks burned, but he was determined to prove the captain wrong.

At the end of the first week, he caught the captain watching him as he helped dig a trench under the roasting sun.

"Good work, son," Captain Marsh said, with the flicker of an almost-smile.

Nate felt like he'd won a medal.

Nate missed Eliza and Theo. But he soon felt at home in the camp. The eighty men of the Connecticut 5th welcomed him. Paul hardly let Nate out of his sight. A few of the other men kept their eyes on Nate, too.

The oldest of the group was Samuel. He was fifty-three — ancient! But he was strong and fast and the best shooter of the group.

There was James, the youngest of the soldiers. He came from a rich family — the other men made fun of the silver buckles on his boots. But James wasn't all fancy. He had the loudest burp of the bunch. He was always leaving little gifts in Nate's tent — a pair of wool socks, a tin canteen. He even managed to get Nate a frontier shirt, one of the tie-front shirts most of the men in the army wore with pride. Nate was happy to throw away the rough, stained shirt he'd been wearing for months.

Another man who looked after Nate was Martin. He cleaned and bandaged Nate's blistered hands and patched up the holes in the bottom of his boots. Up until a few months ago, Martin had been a slave. His owner had freed him so he could fight in the war. But that same man had refused to free Martin's wife and daughter. Now Martin hoped his meager soldiers' pay would help him save up to buy freedom for his family.

There were a few hundred other black soldiers in the army. Many more worked in the camp. They were mostly slaves, sent by their masters to dig trenches and build walls. Watching those men work gave Nate an uneasy feeling — like he'd bitten into something rotten, something he couldn't spit out or swallow.

He'd learned more about the Declaration of Independence. It said that all men were created equal. Why didn't that include people like Martin's wife, like those men digging trenches for George Washington, like Eliza and Theo?

Trying to answer that question was like looking for buried treasure without a map. Nate searched his mind for an answer, but he couldn't find it anywhere.

When Nate wasn't busy with his chores, he sometimes watched the men do their practice drills. They'd march through the streets to the different drum songs. Those drums songs weren't for fun. In a noisy battle, the officers couldn't just shout out their orders; their voices would be drowned out by the explosions. It was those different *rat, tat, tat*s that told the men which way to turn, how fast to march, when to load their muskets, and when to shoot.

When they were done marching, the men would practice loading their muskets quickly, which seemed to Nate to be the hardest part of being a soldier. One mistake and the musket could blow up your hand. The ammunition came wrapped in little paper packets called cartridges. Inside was a single musket ball and just enough gunpowder for one shot. The men had to tear those packets open with their teeth.

And, boy, was it hard to get the muskets to fire right! No wonder Paul almost blew his hand off when he was learning.

Of course, Nate didn't have a musket. But Samuel was determined to teach him how to load and fire one perfectly. He spent hours teaching Nate how to pour in the gunpowder. He showed him the right way to ram the musket ball down the gun's barrel. Samuel couldn't let Nate actually shoot — gunpowder was too precious to waste on an eleven-year-old.

MORTAR

HOWITZER

WEAPONS OF THE REVOLUTIONARY WAR

MUSKET

PISTOL

CANNON

BAYONET

SPONTOON

TOMAHAWK

SABER

DAGGER

At the end of the long days, when the marching and musket practice were done, the men could relax by the camp's big fire. And these were Nate's favorite times.

The men would trade battle stories. They'd show off their scars — thighs chewed up by musket balls, bellies and backs clawed by bayonets.

They'd raise up their tin cups of warm water with molasses. And they'd cheer the brave leaders whose words had sparked this fight for freedom.

"To John Adams!"

"To Dr. Warren!"

"To Samuel Adams!"

"To Paul Revere!"

But they saved their loudest cheers for their commander, General George Washington.

Nate saw the general often. He'd ride by the camp on his gray stallion. He was very tall, and always wore an elegant blue uniform with silver buttons and a bright white sash across his chest.

He looked almost kingly, Nate thought. But

the men said he worked as hard as a common soldier.

"To General Washington!" the men would sing. "God save the United States of America!"

Those cheers rang through Nate's mind as he lay in his tent at night.

But some nights Nate woke up to a different sound. It came from his nightmares.

RAT, tat, tat, tat, tat.

RAT, tat, tat, tat, tat.

On those nights it would take a very long time for Nate to fall back to sleep.

CHAPTER 12

By the second week of August, there were about twenty thousand American soldiers in the camps in and around New York City, with more arriving every day. The Americans had built ten big forts on Manhattan Island, and six more across the river in Brooklyn. Each fort had a rough building surrounded by tall dirt-and-stone walls and deep trenches. The walls were topped with cannons.

The men felt ready for battle.

But still the British didn't attack.

Rumors swirled. They heard about a new kind of cannonball called a shell. It exploded when it hit the ground. Spies reported that there were now more than 430 British ships anchored off nearby Staten Island, and at least forty thousand soldiers.

And not all of them were Redcoats.

King George had hired eight thousand German soldiers to fight alongside the British. They were known as Hessians.

Hessians!

The men whispered the word, like it was a curse.

"They're professional killers from Germany," Paul explained.

Hessians were famous around the world for their dark green-and-red uniforms, their pointed silver hats, their thick black mustaches — and their thirst for blood. They began training when they were five years old. They fought mostly with their bayonets, which were twice as long as the ones the British used.

SOLDIERS OF THE AMERICAN REVOLUTION

AS OF 1776

AMERICAN OFFICER

AMERICAN SOLDIER

AMERICAN DRUMMER BOY

HESSIAN SOLDIER

BRITISH SOLDIER

BRITISH DRUMMER BOY

Nate couldn't tell if the stories were completely true. He thought of the legends Papa and the men used to tell, about giant squid and whales that swallowed ships. The Hessians sounded more like storybook monsters than real-life soldiers. But there was no mistaking the fear in the men's eyes.

But there was something even more dangerous than Hessians, and it was lurking right in the camp. Nate discovered it on a boiling afternoon.

The men were on a marching drill, and Nate was alone in the camp doing his chores. The weather was beastly hot. The sun beat down. Mosquitos attacked them at night. And the usual camp smells turned into an unbearable stink.

The most stomach-turning odors rose up from the open latrine pits where the men — and Nate — all did their private business. Some days Nate felt sure his nose would burn right off.

Nate was taking a break from chopping wood. He took a swig from the tin canteen James had given him.

And then he heard a strange sound, like an animal was crying out in pain.

Nate looked around, thinking it was one of the cats that chased rats around the camp.

He heard the sound again, and he realized it was coming from inside one of the tents.

It was James's tent.

Nate remembered that James had been ill yesterday. There were always gut sicknesses and fevers sweeping through the camp. Nate figured James had one of those.

Nate stood outside the tent.

"James?" he said. "It's Nate. Are you all right?"

Silence. More moaning. Nate's heart pounded as he stuck his head through the tent flap. And then he lurched back in horror.

There was someone on the ground — it had to be James. Except it didn't look like James — or even a human being. Hundreds and hundreds of hideous blisters boiled all over his face. His arms and chest were covered, too.

It was smallpox, the most dreaded disease of all.

It was the disease that stole Nate's mama all those years ago. It had almost killed Nate, too.

Nate pushed away his fear and disgust. He went inside and knelt next to James. He took James's hand. It was burning hot.

"James," Nate said, swallowing the lump in his throat.

"Go away," James rasped. "You'll get sick."

"I had it already," Nate said, taking the young man's hand. Having smallpox once — if it didn't kill you — meant you couldn't get it again. Almost half the people who got the disease died. Some came through, but were badly scarred. Eliza had scars on her cheeks. Theo had them all over his back.

Nate didn't need a doctor to tell him that James was dying.

He said a prayer and then rushed to find help.

He returned with Paul and Martin, who were both safe from smallpox.

Nate helped them bring James to the hospital. James died that night.

Captain Marsh led a service for him. All of the men shed tears for that kind and generous man.

The weeks ticked by. Nate became more and more restless. He worried that other men would get sick. He kept thinking of Papa. He missed Eliza and Theo. These thoughts weighed down on him, like rocks in his pockets.

The mood of the camp grew darker.

And then, on the afternoon of August 21, the sky suddenly turned black. And New York City was slammed by a thunderstorm more violent than even the storm that took Papa.

Rain poured down. The howling wind ripped apart tents, knocked over trees, and sent barrels flying through the air.

But most terrifying was the lightning. Blinding bolts stabbed down like Hessian bayonets. At a camp nearer to the river, ten soldiers were struck dead by a single bolt. Three other soldiers were hit as they were running along the street. The lightning killed the men and melted the coins in their pockets.

Nate lay awake all night as the storm raged.

He had the feeling that the furious wind was screaming out a warning.

And it was.

The next morning, word came that the British were on the move. Thousands of British troops had landed on Brooklyn, just across the East River from New York City.

The British attack was about to begin.

CHAPTER 13

AUGUST 25, 1776
10:00 A.M.
BROOKLYN

Three days later the Connecticut 5th was ordered to Brooklyn along with six thousand other soldiers. They were all ferried across the East River on big rowboats. Nate and the men were sent to Fort Greene, one of the six Brooklyn forts. All of the forts were spread across Brooklyn Heights. That was the part of Brooklyn that was closest to New York City.

Nate hadn't realized how huge Brooklyn was. It had to be at least ten times the size of New York City. And much of the land was wild. Only a few hundred people lived in Brooklyn, and most had fled.

But this wild land was important in the war. If the British took Brooklyn, they would put their cannons on Brooklyn Heights. From there, they could blast New York City to bits.

"But we're not going to let that happen," Captain Marsh said. It was a few hours after they'd arrived at Fort Greene. Nate and the men had set up their tents inside the fort's tall dirt walls. Now Captain Marsh was explaining the American battle plan.

He showed them a map of Brooklyn and pointed out the six American forts. Then Captain Marsh pointed to a squiggly line on the map. It looked to be about one mile from Brooklyn Heights. "That's the Gowanus Heights," he said. It was a long ridge of hills.

"The British are somewhere on the other side of the ridge, and they have to cross the hills of

Gowanus Heights to get to our fort. But we already have three thousand men guarding those hills. When the British try to cross . . ."

Paul chimed in. "We'll blast them right back to England!"

Captain March cracked a tiny smile. "Or at least back to Staten Island."

The Redcoats and Hessians who made it to the forts would face dozens of cannons. Thousands of Americans would be shooting at them from trenches, protected by the tall dirt walls.

"It will be like Bunker Hill," Samuel said with a hopeful smile.

"That's right," Captain Marsh said, the certainty gleaming in his eyes. The men cheered.

Several nights passed, and Brooklyn stayed mostly quiet.

On the night of August 26, soldiers from different companies gathered around the campfires. They roasted hunks of pork on sharpened sticks. They insulted the British and called the Hessians foul names Nate would never repeat.

To Nate, it almost seemed that the men were looking forward to a big party, not a bloody battle.

They sang songs, including one that Nate had never heard before. It had a bright and catchy tune, but words that made no sense at all.

Yankee Doodle went to town, riding on a pony . . .

One man played along on a little twinkling flute called a fife.

Paul, Martin, and Samuel all sang along.

Yankee Doodle, keep it up, Yankee Doodle Dandy . . .

"What's a Yankee Doodle?" Nate asked, raising his voice up over the singing and knee slapping.

"It's what the British call us," Martin said. "They say the Americans are a bunch of Yankee Doodles, country fools who don't know how to fight."

"The British made up this song, to tease us in battle," Paul added.

"So why are *we* singing it?" Nate asked.

This made no sense at all.

"Because at Bunker Hill, we showed them what a bunch of Yankee Doodles can do," Samuel said. "We stole the name — and the song."

Nate smiled. Now he got it.

The Americans took the British insult — and turned it into a battle song.

The singing went on until a blaring trumpet called the men to attention.

Three men appeared. The man in the center was very tall and wore a blue uniform. The men leaped to their feet.

It was General Washington!

The general stood quietly for a moment, as the men gathered around him. A hush came over the camp. Even the grumpiest and sleepiest of the men stood up straight. They brushed the dust from their shirts and straightened their caps. Nate stood extra tall.

"The moment has come," General Washington began. "The enemy has landed. And now the honor and success of America depends on you."

His voice was calm but powerful.

He told them that a great battle was coming. He reminded the men what they were fighting for — for freedom, for their new country.

"The world will soon learn what a few brave men, fighting for their own land, can do."

His words seemed to rise up into the air. And Nate knew he'd never forget the sound of the general's voice. Most of all, Nate would remember the feeling of being almost lifted up off the ground, by nothing more than words.

General Washington didn't speak for long. But

even hours later, his voice seemed to echo through the camp.

After the general left, the men settled down in their tents. Nate quickly fell asleep.

Just after dawn, the sound of American alarm cannons boomed through the fort.

Paul poked his head into Nate's tent. His eyes were flashing with excitement.

"The British are trying to cross the Gowanus Heights!"

The Battle of Brooklyn was about to begin.

CHAPTER 14

AUGUST 27
9:00 A.M.
BROOKLYN, NEW YORK

The men of the Connecticut 5th were ordered to help guard the Gowanus Heights.

Days before, Captain Marsh had told Nate that he would stay inside the fort for as long as they were in Brooklyn.

"You're not a soldier," he'd said. "I don't want you on the battlefield."

But that morning, twenty-two men in the Connecticut 5th were too sick to march. There were not enough men to carry ammunition and other supplies to the ridge.

"Nate," the captain said. "I need you to march with us to the camp. And then you'll return here to the fort."

They were taking the place of some Pennsylvania soldiers who had been on duty there for three days straight.

"You'll march back here with the Pennsylvania men."

"Yes, sir," Nate said.

"Anything happens, we all get ourselves back to the fort. You hear?"

"Yes, sir."

Gruesome pictures flashed through Nate's mind as he thought of stepping out of the fort. Exploding cannonballs. Gut-smashing musket balls. Bayonets dripping with blood.

But a rush of pride swept Nate's fears away. Captain Marsh was counting on Nate.

Paul helped Nate load up a large knapsack with extra ammunition cartridges. He was unusually quiet. He didn't like the idea of Nate leaving the fort.

"You follow me," Paul said as they were lining up. "And stay close."

Nate nodded.

He took a place in line between Paul and Samuel.

And they all set out into the wilds of Brooklyn.

They marched along a narrow road, under a sunny sky. The road cut through fields and meadows. They passed a deserted farm. The house was boarded up and there was not a person or animal in sight. In the yard was a big tree, with a wooden swing hanging from a branch. Nate could imagine Theo shrieking happily as he flew up and down.

Nate felt the familiar ache of missing Theo. He also thought about the family that had built up that farm. Where had they all gone? Would they ever be able to come back?

For the first time it really hit Nate: This war wasn't just about King George and soldiers on battlefields. Regular people would lose their homes. Others would lose far more — their family members and friends. Even if the Americans won, some people would never be able to get back what they had lost.

The road took them up a hill, and soon they were in the woods.

They had reached the Gowanus Heights. There were groups of American soldiers standing guard along the way, but not as many as Nate would have expected. They turned off the road and walked along the ridge. The thickening woods made it hard to see more than just a few yards ahead. All was very quiet.

And then . . .

Boom!

Boom!

Two sharp cannon blasts shook the ground.

Nate froze. Samuel whipped around.

"That's strange," he said, his eyes narrowed with worry. "Those cannons were shot from *this* side of the ridge."

Samuel scanned the woods.

"The Americans don't have big cannons this far from the forts. The British aren't supposed to be anywhere near here."

But they were. And they had the high ground!

KI-crack! KI-crack! KI-crack! KI-crack!

Musket fire blasted them from the hill just above.

Hissssssss!

A ball streaked right by Nate's ear.

Looking up, Nate saw splashes of red between the trees up on the hill.

Redcoats!

"Take cover!" Captain Marsh shouted.

Nate threw himself down into the dirt and covered his head with his hands.

More shots exploded.

KI-crack!

Hissssss!

Samuel cried out. Nate peeked up just in time to see him crumple to his knees. Samuel's hands flew up to his chest. Blood gushed from between his fingers.

Nate saw it all so clearly. But he couldn't believe it was happening. All he could think was *no.*

No, no, no, no.

The life drained from Samuel's face. His body seemed to melt to the ground.

Nate sprang up and rushed for Samuel. But the Redcoats were shooting again.

KI-crack!

Hissssss!

Nate dove back behind the tree.

Captain Marsh's voice shouted out orders.

"Prepare!"

The Connecticut 5th men aimed their muskets.

KI-crack! KI-crack! KI-crack! KI-crack!

Then they dropped to their knees and reloaded, exactly as they had practiced in their drills.

But this was not a drill.

Nate shook himself out of his shock.

Samuel's musket was lying on the ground. He'd spent hours teaching Nate how to use it. And now Nate knew what Samuel would expect him to do.

Nate grabbed the musket.

The wooden handle was still warm from Samuel's hands.

CHAPTER 15

Nate took off his big knapsack and grabbed some ammunition cartridges. He stuffed them into his pockets. Then he crawled back to his tree.

He held his weapon like Samuel had showed him, and aimed up the hill. He could see the soldiers in their bloodred coats hiding in the trees. It looked like only about twenty men. Probably soldiers sent ahead as scouts.

He waited for Captain Marsh's orders.

"Pre-sent!" Captain Marsh shouted.

Nate clicked back the flintlock, holding his aim.

"Fire!"

Nate pulled the trigger.

KI-crack!

The gunpowder exploded inside the gun. The musket ball streaked out of the barrel like a comet, trailing flames and smoke. The other men shot at the same time. And Nate's musket ball joined theirs in the blizzard of metal sweeping up the hill.

The Redcoats scattered.

Nate and the men all reloaded. He aimed again, ready to shoot. But the Redcoats didn't come back.

They all waited for them to return. Minutes ticked by. Finally Captain Marsh gave the order for them to line up again.

"We need to get to our camp, men!" he shouted.

Nate stood up.

"Captain!" he called. "It's Samuel, sir."

A moment later all of the men were gathered around Samuel's body.

Martin knelt down and put his hand on Samuel's blood-soaked chest.

He looked up at Captain Marsh. "He's gone, sir."

Captain Marsh's stony face seemed to crumble for a moment, and then he regained his steely determination.

The men all said a prayer. And then they stood silently.

But then a chilling song shattered the moment.

RAT, tat, tat, tat, tat.

RAT, tat, tat, tat, tat.

Battle drums, like from Nate's nightmare.

Except these were real.

The sound got louder.

Rat, tat, tat, tat, tat.

Rat, tat, tat, tat, tat.

Rat, tat, tat, tat, tat.

"What will we do, captain?" Paul asked.

Paul had an unusual look in his eyes, one that Nate had seen only once before: during the storm that took Papa.

It was fear.

"We need to get back to the fort," Captain Marsh said.

But it was too late. Before they could take a step, the ground started to shake. It sounded like a stampede of giants was heading right for them.

And in a way, that was exactly what was happening. Suddenly hundreds of soldiers were charging over the top of the ridge.

They were not Redcoats.

They were not American.

They wore dark green-and-red uniforms and tall, pointed silver hats.

They carried muskets topped with long glinting bayonets.

Hessians!

The hillside exploded into a wall of flames and gunpowder smoke.

Balls hissed by, smacking into the trees and cutting holes in the ground.

And this time there was no way for the men of the Connecticut 5th to shoot back.

The Hessians were pouring over the hills, like a churning wave of green and red and silver.

"Retreat!" Captain Marsh bellowed.

The men scattered in different directions.

Paul grabbed Nate by the arm and they tore through the woods.

Cannon blasts rang out.

Boom!

Boom!

That evil sizzling sound of approaching cannonballs filled the air.

Crash!

A cannonball shattered a tree right in front of them. Shards of wood flew like daggers.

A sharp piece hit Nate on the cheek, an inch from his eye. Paul lost his grip on Nate.

The smoke was so thick now. Nate could hardly see. He lost Paul and ran almost blindly, stumbling over rocks and weaving around trees.

Musket balls whizzed by.

Nate heard footsteps behind him.

Paul!

But when he looked over his shoulder he didn't see his friend. Instead he saw a man in a silver hat — a Hessian. He was chasing after Nate with his bayonet held straight out in front of him, shouting angrily in a language Nate had never

heard. But Nate did not need to understand the words. Even through the smoke, Nate could see the hatred and fury in the man's eyes.

Nate wanted to scream, "I'm not a soldier!

But it didn't matter that Nate was just an eleven-year-old boy. That Hessian meant to kill him.

Nate's legs were giving out. He was slowing down. He braced for the vicious stab, for the agonizing pain, for the end.

But then a cannonball sizzled overhead.

And it wasn't a regular cannonball. It was an exploding shell.

Kaboom!

The world around Nate seemed to shatter apart. And then, *whoosh!* In the same instant, Nate was ripped up off the ground.

There was searing heat. Blinding light.

And then . . . darkness.

CHAPTER 16

2 HOURS LATER

Nate opened his eyes.

Where was he? He seemed to be inside a big, deep hole. There was dirt and grass everywhere, even in his mouth.

He must be in his grave! He'd been buried alive!

He sat up, coughing and gasping.

No. This hole was not a grave. And Nate was still alive. Explosions and the smell of gunpowder smoke helped clear his mind. And he remembered. The Redcoat attack. Samuel. Hessians charging over the hill. That grunting soldier with his bayonet. The explosion.

It must have been a shell . . . one of those new exploding cannonballs. It had blasted this crater in the ground. Somehow Nate had tumbled inside it.

Nate struggled to his feet and checked himself from head to toe. His pants were ripped. The cut on his face was oozing blood. He felt like he'd been run over by a horse wagon. But amazingly, he was in one piece.

He spat the dirt from his mouth and turned around, then reeled back in fear.

There was a hand — a bloody hand — hanging over the edge of the crater. Nate crept closer until he could see that the hand was attached to a man — the Hessian.

The soldier was splayed out on his back, with one leg twisted in a way it shouldn't be. His silver cap was next to him, the musket and bayonet near his feet.

His eyes were opened wide, unblinking.

He was dead.

Nate wanted to turn away, but he couldn't. The Hessian's eyes seemed to grab hold of Nate's, forcing him to look. He was very young, Nate could see, around Paul's age. He didn't look like a bloodthirsty killer anymore. He looked like someone's son, an older brother. Nate stood there until finally a cannon blast from somewhere very close jolted him out of his trance. The battle was still raging. He felt like he'd woken up from one nightmare, only to be locked inside a new one. Cannons and musket fire seemed to be crackling on both sides of him. The air was thick with smoke.

What had happened to Paul and the men? How would Nate get back to the fort on Brooklyn Heights? That's what Captain Marsh had told him to do. But how? He couldn't just stroll through the woods. There were Redcoats and Hessians everywhere. Nate might not be a real soldier, but he sure looked like one. He was tall for his age. He was wearing the frontier shirt that James had given him. He looked like any young American soldier, desperate to escape.

Terrifying thoughts screamed through his mind.

He'd be shot!

Crushed by a cannonball!

He'd be caught and locked away in a rat-filled British prison.

The men had told terrible stories about how the British treated their American prisoners. They crammed them into filthy basements or old, rotting ships. Most men died slowly of starvation or fevers. Paul said he'd rather get shot on the battlefield than starve to death in a British prison.

Nate started to shake. He looked at the big hole in the ground. Maybe he should just climb back down and curl up into a ball.

What else could he do?

And then, once again, his mind flashed to the pirate Slash O'Shea. He remembered a story Papa had told him, about a time Slash was in London. He'd been working as a pirate for a few years. He'd come ashore to hand out gold coins to poor kids on the streets. A policeman spotted

Slash and started to chase him. Slash managed to duck into a tavern. Inside was a man wearing a fancy blue velvet coat and a top hat.

Slash dug into his pockets and pulled out a handful of gold coins. He slapped them on the table in front of the man.

"For your coat and hat!"

A minute later, Slash was strolling out of the tavern in that fancy outfit.

He strolled right past a group of policemen, tipping his hat like a gentleman.

Slash escaped from London that night, and was soon back at sea.

Nate looked at the Hessian, lying on the ground, and he knew what to do.

He knelt down and unbuttoned the brass buttons of the green coat. It was wrong to steal from a dead man. But this dead man had tried to kill him.

Nate carefully slipped the coat off the man's body. He shook it out and tried it on.

It hung down past Nate's knees.

But Nate could easily fix that. He shrugged it off, and used the Hessian's razor-sharp bayonet to help him tear off the bottom of the coat. He tried it on again.

Better. Next he put on the helmet. He had to push it back so it didn't cover his eyes. Finally he picked up the Hessian's musket and bayonet and put it over his shoulder.

Nate stood there, too scared to move.

He just had to get out of the woods and across the field to the fort. It was only about a mile from here, Nate guessed. If he walked quickly, he'd be back inside the fort in fifteen minutes.

But looking ahead, Nate felt like he had to cross an ocean.

Without a boat.

In a storm.

By himself.

He closed his eyes, and there it was: the feeling of Papa's hand on his shoulder. He moved his fingers, and imagined Eliza's hand in his.

And he started walking.

CHAPTER 17

Nate moved slowly through the forest, his eyes scanning, his ears open for pounding footsteps and evil cannonball sizzles and musket ball hisses. Explosions and musket cracks filled the air. But the sky over the forts was still clear of smoke. Nate hoped that meant that the British had not made it that far.

Nate passed two soldiers, both dead from musket shots. One was an American, about Papa's age. The other was a young Redcoat. Nate whispered prayers as he went by each one.

He kept moving. He saw no more soldiers — alive or dead.

But a few minutes later he heard voices.

There, not far ahead, up in the hills. Four Redcoats.

Every one of Nate's muscles twitched.

Run!

But Nate thought of Slash, tipping his hat at the policemen as he strolled by.

Nate reminded himself: He was not a terrified young boy. He was a brave Hessian! Hopefully the soldiers were far enough away so they wouldn't notice the coat's torn bottom and how it sagged off Nate's shoulders.

Nate gritted his teeth. He walked along, waving stiffly like a Hessian might.

To Nate's shock, the Redcoats waved back.

Soon they were out of sight. And Nate made it to the road. It would lead him out of the woods and right back to the fort.

Nate quickened his steps.

Explosions pounded his ears. Smoke burned

his eyes and nose. The booms and crackles were getting louder.

Just get to the fort, Nate told himself. *Just get to the fort.*

He came to the edge of the woods. Now just about half a mile of open fields stood between him and his fort on Brooklyn Heights. The Americans had a wide-open view of anyone approaching the forts. They'd see Nate and think he was a Hessian. They might shoot him by mistake. Nate quickly ripped off the coat and silver hat and tossed them into a bush, along with the musket and bayonet.

He had taken just a few steps when he heard that nightmarish sound.

RAT, tat, tat, tat, tat.

RAT, tat, tat, tat, tat.

Nate looked slowly to his right. And what he saw in the distance turned his blood to ice.

There were thousands of men, a sea of bright red spreading as far back as Nate could see.

RAT, tat, tat, tat, tat.

RAT, tat, tat, tat, tat.

Before Nate could figure out what to do, he heard pounding footsteps and panicked voices coming from the woods behind him.

"They're coming!"

"They're right behind us!"

"Get to the fort!"

Men burst out of the woods — dozens and dozens of American soldiers running for their lives. Some were bloodied. All wore wild looks of fear. Before Nate knew it, he was running, too.

He glanced behind him, and saw some Redcoats and Hessians trying to catch up.

And to the right, that huge Redcoat army was on the march.

Their drums beat louder.

RAT, tat, tat, tat, tat.

Shots rang out. Cannons boomed. Balls whizzed by.

Nate tried not to imagine the blinding pain of his guts being torn open, his bones splintering, his clothes soaked with blood. Any minute he expected a cannonball to plow through the crowd, for an explosion to blow them all into the smoky sky.

Kaboom!

Kaboom!

KI-crack! KI-crack!

Sizzle.

Hiss.

The sounds all melded together — the explosions, the shouts, the footsteps, the pounding of Nate's heart. It was like the night of the storm that had taken Papa, a wild swirl of terror.

But Nate was not hit.

And there was the fort, with hundreds of American soldiers waiting for them. Nate ran with the crowd to the back of the fort, where there was a small break in the wall.

He collapsed onto the ground. But he sat there just long enough to catch his breath. And then he walked all around the fort, searching the crowd of dazed and terrified men for Paul, Martin, Captain Marsh, and the rest of the Connecticut 5th.

They were nowhere to be found.

Reports trickled in from the hideous battle raging outside.

Hundreds of Americans had been killed and

captured already. British and Hessian soldiers were getting closer to the fort.

The attack would be brutal.

The Americans were doomed.

Hours crawled by. More and more American soldiers staggered in. Many were covered with mud from escapes through swamps. Others were soaking wet and half-drowned from swimming across ponds and creeks. Some clutched arms that had been shattered by British or Hessian musket balls. Others were bleeding from the bayonet gashes.

Dawn came, and still the British didn't attack. Some said they were waiting until they could sail their warships into the East River. This would let them attack from two sides, and stop the Americans from trying to escape back to New York City.

American soldiers stood at attention in their trenches. The cannons were loaded and ready to blast. It seemed like everyone in the fort was holding his breath, waiting.

Meanwhile, all Nate could think about was the men of the Connecticut 5th.

Just before dawn, the skies opened. It rained all day, soaking the men and turning the fort into a sea of mud. But Nate barely noticed the cold rain and wind. He stood outside all day, shivering and waiting.

It wasn't until the late afternoon that a last group of American soldiers made it to Fort Greene.

Their clothes were tattered. Their faces were caked with dirt. But there was no mistaking the man in the hideous green hat.

Nate's heart leaped.

Paul and the men of the Connecticut 5th had made it back.

CHAPTER 18

6 MONTHS LATER
FEBRUARY 2, 1777
2:00 P.M.

Nate walked quickly along the quiet dirt road. It was very cold, but the sun was warm on his back. He'd been traveling for three days. He'd journeyed first by boat, then by wagon. Now he was on foot. Very soon his long journey would be over.

Nate's mind was filled up with memories of all that had happened to him over these past seven months. He thought of the scared and lonely boy who had run away from Storch's house. Had that really been Nate? Somehow he'd left that boy behind, maybe in that bloody forest in Brooklyn.

Oh, that terrible battle!

What a disaster it had been for the Americans. The British had outmanned them, outgunned them, and outsmarted them. Hundreds of Americans had been killed. Many more had been injured and captured. It could have been far worse. The British could have captured most of the American army, including General Washington!

But they kept delaying their attack on the American forts. The stormy weather kept the big British warships from laying their trap in the East River. The delay gave General Washington a chance to pull off a miracle. On the dark and foggy night of August 27, almost ten thousand American troops snuck off Brooklyn in a fleet of small boats. They made it safely back to New York City. When the British finally attacked the forts, they found them empty.

Most of the American army had managed to survive the Battle of Brooklyn.

But General Washington's troubles were just beginning.

Within weeks, the British had attacked New York City. By the end of November, all of Manhattan Island was in British hands.

America's fight for freedom was melting away. Soldiers fled the army until there were only about three thousand men left. The Connecticut 5th had dwindled down to just thirty men.

But Paul never gave up hope.

And neither did General Washington.

On December 26, the Americans launched a surprise attack on a Hessian camp in Trenton, New Jersey. A week later, the Americans battled the British in Princeton, New Jersey — and won. Those small victories put the spirit back into the American fight. Even Captain Marsh smiled a little.

Nate had planned to stay with the Connecticut 5th. He'd moved with them to the American army's winter camp, in Morristown, New Jersey.

But then, just seven days ago, Nate had received a letter. It was from Mr. Marston, Storch's friend.

Somehow word must have gotten back to Norwalk that Nate was in the Connecticut 5th. Mr. Marston had managed to track Nate down.

Nothing could have prepared Nate for what that letter said.

Storch was dead, of smallpox. Returning American soldiers had brought the disease back to Norwalk. More than one hundred people had died.

But the truly shocking news came at the end of the letter.

Mr. Marston explained that Storch had left no will — no letter saying what should be done with his property.

You are your uncle's only living family member. Because he left no will, all of your uncle's assests go to you.

Nate read that sentence about twenty times until he fully understood what this meant for him — and for Eliza and Theo.

They could be free. That's why Nate was heading back to Norwalk. So he could get Eliza and Theo their freedom papers.

Captain Marsh, Martin, and Paul had helped Nate plan his trip back to Norwalk. They'd hugged him good-bye, even Captain Marsh. Paul took his ugly green hat and put it onto Nate's head, to bring him luck.

"You better come back soon!" Paul had said, the flash in his eyes brighter than ever. "We're going to win this fight!"

Nate didn't doubt it. The Americans would keep fighting for as long as it took. But for now, at least, Nate's army days were over. He'd seen enough blood. His dreams were filled with horror — of unblinking Hessian eyes, Samuel's body crumpled on the ground, the explosions of cannons and muskets.

And he never stopped hearing those British battle drums, that ghostly *RAT, tat, tat, tat, tat.* Even when he was awake that terrible rattle echoed through his mind.

Nate walked more quickly now. He could see the roof of the house in the distance.

What would happen next? Eliza would have plans of her own. She'd want to find her husband,

Gregory. Maybe Theo could go to school. As for Nate, he wasn't sure. Papa had been right: You never knew what was ahead in life. And these past seven months had taught Nate something else: that nothing was impossible.

A group of ragtag soldiers could take on the most powerful country in the world.

One man's words could lift a thousand soldiers right up off the ground.

A terrified boy could become a brave American fighter.

And just ahead, the most impossibly happy sight of all: Eliza and Theo, standing under the cherry tree.

Nate started to run toward them. His knapsack slipped off, but he didn't stop.

For the first time in months, the *RAT, tat, tat, tat, tat* of war faded from his mind.

All Nate could hear now was Theo's voice, joyfully shouting out his name.

A FASCINATING
RESEARCH JOURNEY

Dear Readers,

I'm writing to you on my laptop computer from my office in Connecticut. I'm wearing a pair of red sweatpants and munching on potato chips.

But in my mind, I am still in colonial New York City. Instead of a computer, I'm scribbling away with my feather quill dipped in ink. I'm wearing a long flowered dress and a white bonnet (very flattering!). I'm chewing on some roasted ox.

Every I Survived book takes me on a journey through time. But the journey for this book has been especially long and thrilling. It's taking me a little longer than usual to feel like I'm back home.

For years I Survived readers have been suggesting a book about the Revolutionary War. But the war was long — it lasted from 1775 to 1783. I wasn't sure what to focus on. I knew I would have to do an enormous amount of research to understand this complex event.

And so I kept avoiding the topic.

Then one day I was at a park in Fort Greene, Brooklyn. There's a huge monument there — a towering column topped by a metal sculpture. I was shocked to learn that it was dedicated to Revolutionary War soldiers who died on British prison ships.

British prison ships?

I sat down on a bench and did some instant research. I learned that 11,500 American soldiers died on prison ships docked in the waters around Brooklyn. Many of them were captured during the Battle of Brooklyn (also known as the Battle of Long Island), the biggest battle of the Revolutionary War.

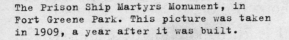

The Prison Ship Martyrs Monument, in
Fort Greene Park. This picture was taken
in 1909, a year after it was built.

I was even more shocked. I had never heard of
the Battle of Brooklyn. It turned out that most
people I knew hadn't heard of it, either.

I knew I had the topic for my book about the
Revolutionary War.

That trip to the Brooklyn park began a research
project that included reading about thirty books,
plus dozens of letters, diary entries, and battle
reports written in 1776. I went to Brooklyn,

Mount Vernon, Boston, and two Pennsylvania battlefields. I learned how to fire a musket (on YouTube). I picked up a cannonball (at a museum in Brooklyn). I interviewed historians.

I learned that the Revolutionary War was far more terrifying, complicated, messy, and miraculous than I'd ever imagined. I spent more than six months researching this topic, and for the entire time I felt a sense of wonder and fascination.

I hope I have captured some of that in this book. And I hope my one small story inspires you to begin your own journey learning about the Revolutionary War.

I'm happy to be home and with all of you.

As they would have said in 1776:

Huzzah!

MY RESEARCH JOURNEY

I learned so much during my research and couldn't fit most of it into my story. So here are some of the most important and interesting things I uncovered about the American Revolution and this time period.

There had never been a country like the United States of America.

In the 1770s, almost every country in the world was ruled by a king or queen. Those men and women didn't earn their jobs. They were born into them. You had to have "royal blood" to lead a country. And regular people like us? Unless we were super rich, or somehow connected to the king or queen, we were pretty powerless. If we spoke out against our king or queen, we could get into huge trouble (or get our heads chopped off!).

But America's founders — people like John Adams, his cousin Samuel, Ben Franklin, and Dr. Joseph Warren (look him up; he was a good one) — had a very different idea of what a country could be. There would be no kings or queens. The leaders could be regular people (in the beginning that would mean only white men, but more on that later). People would have the right to speak out against their government. Rich men and poor men would be treated the same.

This might not seem so bold. But in the 1770s there was no country like this anywhere on Earth. Many people said a country "of the people" would never work. Even if we won the war, many predicted that the "American experiment" would fail.

There have been many rocky times in our history.

But, more than two hundred and fifty years later, here we are.

I could write fifty books just about the American Revolution.

As I told you before, it wasn't easy for me to figure out what part of the American Revolution to write about. At first it seemed logical to write about the most famous events. Why didn't I write a whole book about Bunker Hill? Why didn't I choose a battle that America won, like the Battles of Saratoga or Yorktown? The answer: I could have — and maybe one day I will.

But I wanted to focus on the year 1776, the year the Declaration of Independence was signed. I wanted to write about events that maybe most people hadn't heard of.

And here's the truth. I knew that no single I Survived book could come close to telling the complete story of the American Revolution. In this book, I wanted you to get a sense of why so many Americans wanted to break away from England, and what a bloody struggle it would be.

George Washington was even more interesting than I knew.

I became more and more impressed with our first president as I researched this book. He was smart. He was brave. He was a great husband and doting father to his stepchildren.

But what I admire most: The guy knew how to fail. He made horrible mistakes. And then he would learn from them.

Like the Battle of Brooklyn.

What a stinking mess that was! The battle was terribly planned. Washington didn't have enough troops. He should have known the American army didn't have a chance. Yes, he pulled off that miraculous retreat. But still, he nearly lost half his army and almost wound up a prisoner of England. The whole war would have ended there.

That battle was humiliating for George Washington. He wrote sad letters to his friends. He knew he had messed up big-time. And he kept messing up, until nearly the end of 1776.

But he didn't quit. He admitted his failures.

And even more: He learned from them. As the months passed by he went from being a bad general to becoming a better general until, by the end of the war, he became a great general.

There are many paintings of George Washington, but this is my favorite. It was painted in 1776, the same year as the Battle of Brooklyn.

The Revolutionary War was a difficult and frightening time in America.

When I used to think of the Revolutionary War, I'd think mainly of brave patriots, proud soldiers, and cheering crowds. There were certainly moments of triumph and celebration. But it was also a time of terrible suffering for many Americans.

The lives of soldiers were harsh, even when they weren't facing cannonballs and musket fire in battle. Those army camps really did stink, and were filled with diseases like smallpox. Often there wasn't enough food. In the winter, some soldiers froze to death.

But the war also brought terror and misery to people up and down the colonies. The British burned many towns, including Fairfield, Connecticut, the town right next to mine. Soldiers brought diseases home from the camps, which killed thousands. Businesses suffered. And of course many people lost family members in the war.

But there was something more, something that I had never thought about. The Revolutionary War didn't just pit America against England. It caused Americans to fight against their fellow Americans. Not everyone supported the idea of an independent America, especially not in the early years of the war. Many Americans felt loyalty to King George (they were known as "Loyalists"). After all, for more than a hundred and fifty years, England had protected its colonies and helped them grow. By 1776, America was one of the richest places in the world. More people knew how to read in America than anywhere else.

But as the war began, Loyalists were condemned — often by their own neighbors. Patriot mobs attacked and tortured Loyalists. Thousands of Loyalists and their families lost their homes and fled to England. Families were torn apart. Lives were shattered.

The Revolutionary War was a LONG war.
The Revolutionary War officially began in Lexington and Concord, on April 19, 1775. The war dragged on for eight years, until September of 1783. In between there were *hundreds* of battles. There was fighting in almost every American colony, from the snowy woods of upstate New York to the steamy swamps of Georgia.

Many of the biggest battles are not well known. The Battle of Brooklyn (also known as the Battle of Long Island) was the largest in terms of the number of soldiers who fought on both sides. The bloodiest was the Battle of Charleston, in South Carolina. In that battle alone, 240 men died or were wounded, and a staggering 7,000 American soldiers were taken prisoner.

Almost every year brought victory and defeat for both sides. America certainly would have lost the war if it hadn't been for a big helping hand from France. In 1778, the French began sending money, troops, and weapons to help the Americans.

Why did the French care about the tiny United States? Mostly because France hated England. France and England were bitter rivals, and the French hoped that losing the thirteen American colonies would make England weaker.

But even after the French stepped in to help, the war dragged on . . . and on. In 1781, the Americans won big in Yorktown, Pennsylvania. But it would still take another two years, and countless battles, to end the war.

And about that line, "all men are created equal . . ."

It is one of the most important lines in the Declaration of Independence: that "all men are created equal."

But what did those words really mean?

They meant all white men were created equal. Black men and American Indians were not included. And women? Definitely not.

Even as Americans were fighting for freedom, hundreds of thousands of people in America were enslaved. Most of them were African

Americans, like Eliza and Theo. In New York City, 20 percent of the people who lived there were slaves. I learned that in my home state, Connecticut, many, many people owned slaves. Slavery was legal in most American states until the 1800s. It wasn't completely outlawed in America until 1865. Thousands of enslaved men fought in the Revolutionary War. Some earned their freedom by fighting. Others did not.

It was painful to read about the lives of enslaved people during the Revolutionary War — and beyond. George Washington, Thomas Jefferson, and Ben Franklin all owned slaves.

How should we think about this?

The truth is, many things in our history are very hard to understand as we look back. Even otherwise smart and honest and kind people did things we think of as evil today.

Some people say we shouldn't talk about these dark subjects. They say that admitting that George Washington owned slaves disrespects his incredible accomplishments.

I don't agree.

Looking honestly at our history is important. We can learn from the mistakes of the people who lived before us. And we can make our country — and ourselves — better and stronger.

I am certain that His Excellency, George Washington would agree with that.

FOR FURTHER READING
AND LEARNING

I read dozens of books while researching this book, including some you will love. Here are a few you should read. They are all historical fiction.

The Seeds of America trilogy, by Laurie Halse Anderson

The Fighting Ground, by Avi

Johnny Tremain, by Esther Forbes

The Keeping Room, by Anna Myers

Woods Runner, by Gary Paulsen

SELECTED BIBLIOGRAPHY

1776, by David McCullough, Simon & Schuster: 1st Paperback edition: 2006

A History of US: From Colonies to Country, 1735–1791, by Joy Hakim, Oxford University Press; 3rd Printing edition: February 3, 2007

A Narrative of a Revolutionary Soldier: Some Adventures, Dangers, and Sufferings, by Joseph Plumb Martin, Signet Classics: June 1, 2010

Boy Soldiers of the American Revolution, by Caroline Cox, The University of North Carolina Press: April 18, 2016

Bunker Hill: A City, A Siege, A Revolution, by Nathaniel Philbrick, Penguin Books; Reprint edition: April 29, 2014

Forgotten Patriots: The Untold Story of American Prisoners During the Revolutionary War, by Edwin G. Burrows, Basic Books; Reprint edition: November 9, 2010

Alexander Hamilton, by Ron Chernow, The Penguin Press: April 26, 2004

New York 1776: The Continentals' first battle, by David Smith, Osprey Publishing; 3rd Printing edition: March 18, 2008

Recollections of Life on the Prison Ship Jersey, by Thomas Dring, Westholme Publishing 2nd edition: November 3, 2010

The Battle for New York: The City at the Heart of the American Revolution, by Barnet Schecter, Walker Books, 1st edition: September 2, 2002

The Battle of Brooklyn 1776, by John J. Gallagher, Da Capo Press: March 2001

Patriots: The Men Who Started the American Revolution, by A. J. Langguth, Simon & Schuster; Trade Paperback edition: March 15, 1989

Washington: A Life, by Ron Chernow, Penguin Books, Paperback edition: September 27, 2011

Washington's Immortals: The Untold Story of an Elite Regiment Who Changed the Course of the Revolution, by Patrick K. O'Donnell, Grove Press, Reprint edition: March 21, 2017

ACKNOWLEDGMENTS

I owe an enormous thank-you to author and historian Barnet Schecter for sharing his deep knowledge of and passion for New York City Revolutionary War history. He made me feel like I traveled back in time to walk the streets of New York City during the summer of 1776. I am grateful for his time, expertise, and his generosity in reviewing this book and helping me straighten out my facts.

Another big thank-you to Hugh Roome, who helped kindle my interest in Revolutionary War New York City through his stories of his own family's fascinating history. Extra thanks for sharing thrilling stories and insights about sailing and maritime history, which helped me envision Papa and Nate's life at sea.

Thank you also to Julie Amitie, Bonnie Cutler, Billy DiMichele, Beth Noble, Kerianne Okie, Charisse Meloto, Monica Palenzuela, Cheryl Weisman, Jeffrey West, and everyone else at Scholastic. And as always, I am grateful to my friend and editor Nancy Mercado for her steadfast patience and kindness through the challenging but ultimately joyful experience of bringing books into the world.